THE
CRAYON

For Erin and Isla

ALADDIN
An imprint of Simon & Schuster Children's Publishing Division
1230 Avenue of the Americas, New York, NY 10020
First Aladdin hardcover edition May 2014
Text and illustrations copyright © 2014 by Simon Rickerty
Originally published in Great Britain in 2013 by Simon & Schuster UK Ltd
All rights reserved, including the right of reproduction in whole or in part in any form.
ALADDIN is a trademark of Simon & Schuster, Inc., and related logo is a registered trademark of Simon & Schuster, Inc.
For information about special discounts for bulk purchases, please contact Simon & Schuster Special Sales at
1-866-506-1949 or business@simonandschuster.com.
The Simon & Schuster Speakers Bureau can bring authors to your live event.
For more information or to book an event contact the Simon & Schuster Speakers Bureau at
1-866-248-3049 or visit our website at www.simonspeakers.com.
Manufactured in China 0214 SUK
10 9 8 7 6 5 4 3 2 1
Full CIP data for this book is available from the Library of Congress.
ISBN 978-1-4814-0475-4 • ISBN 978-1-4814-0476-1 (eBook)

THE CRAYON

Simon Rickerty

ALADDIN

London   New York   Toronto   Sydney   New Delhi

Look!
Blue!

Look!
Red!

Hee hee.

Look what I'm doing!

Blue?
On my side?!

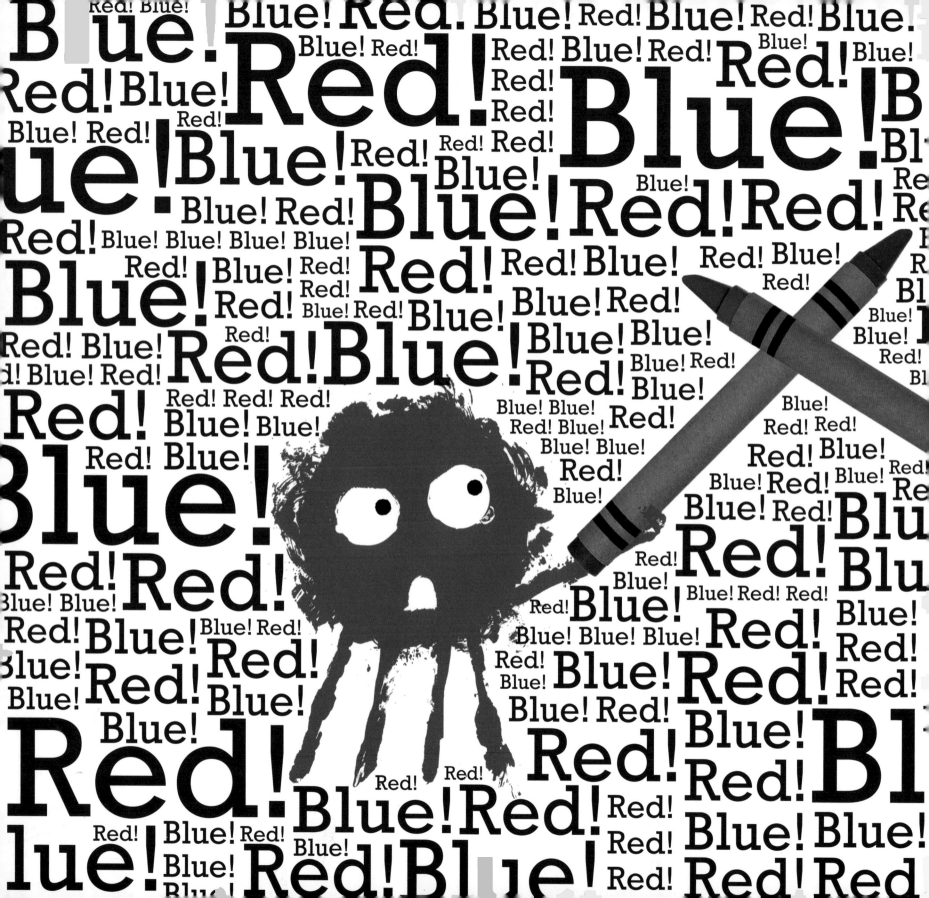

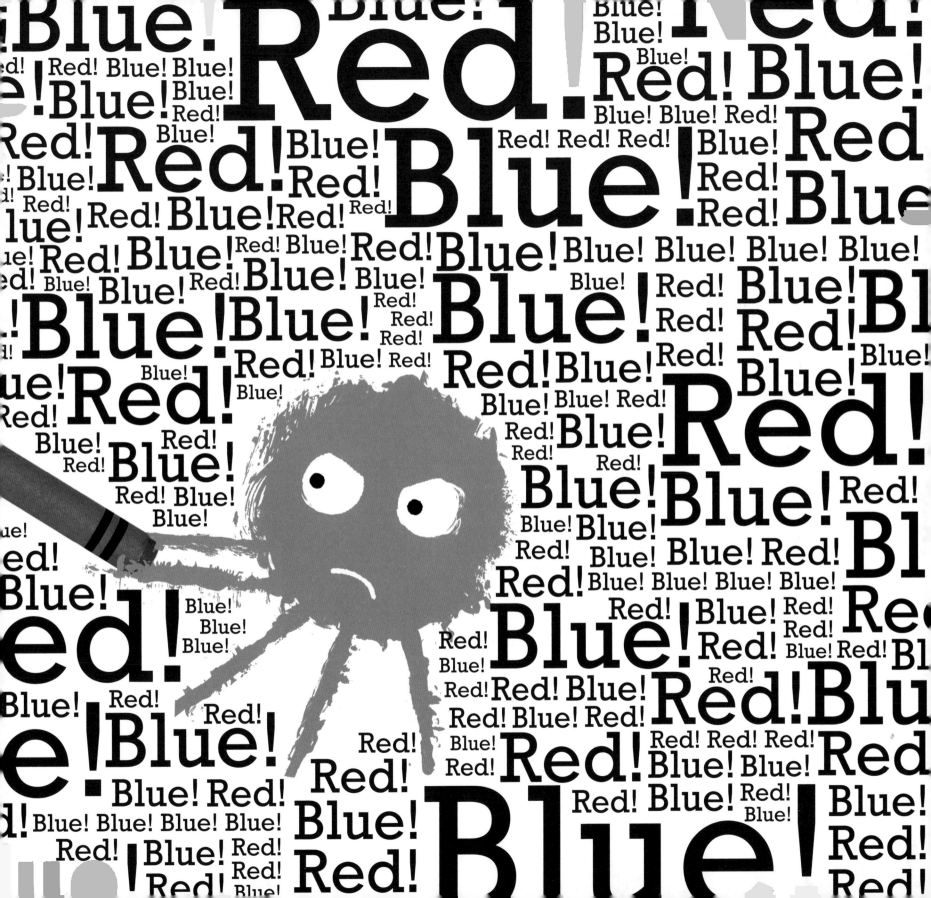

Stop!

Oh.
Oops.

Take my red.

Hee hee!
Now you're . . .

Purple!

Did you
say Purple?

Hey!
Come back!

Wow!

Purple . . .

And
yellow!

And
pink!

Sniff, sniff.

Now for some orange.

A bit of brown.

And green . . .

And now we need . . .

Red!